P9-DUS-689

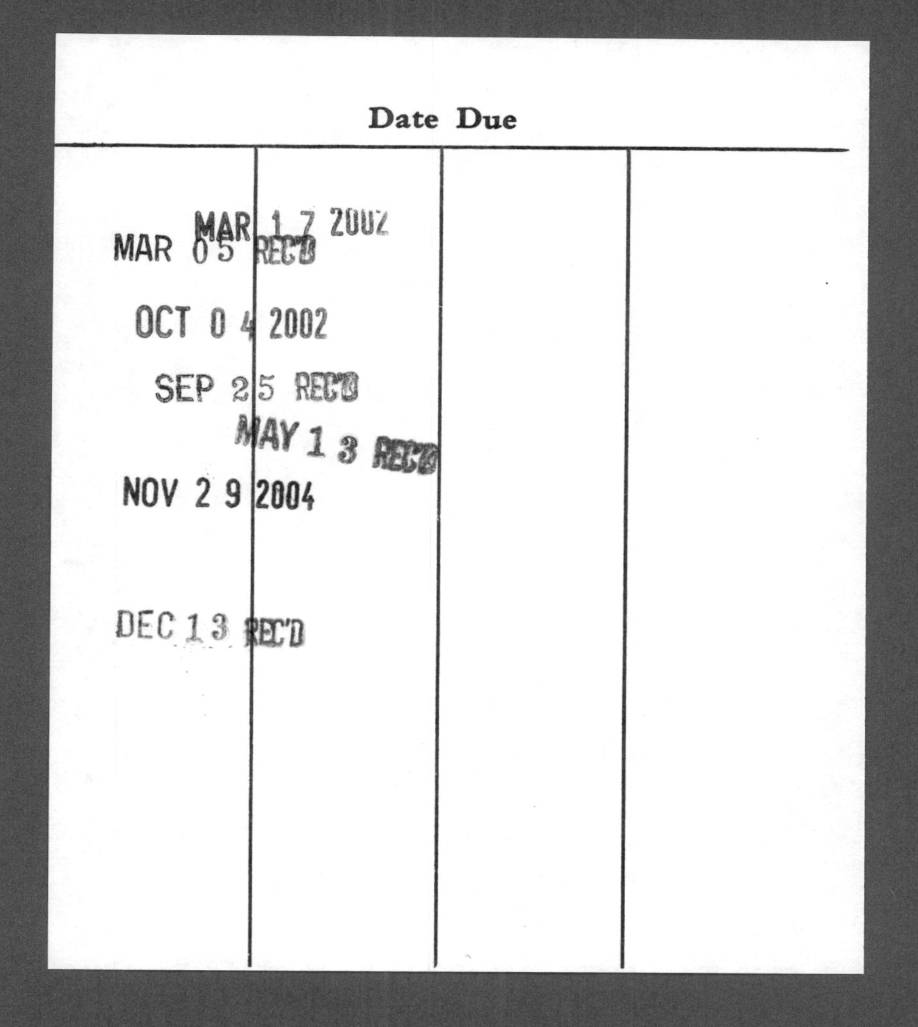
Date Due
MAR 17 2002
MAR 05 REC'D
OCT 04 2002
SEP 25 REC'D
MAY 13 REC'D
NOV 29 2004
DEC 13 REC'D

Today is the day
we are all
going to fly.

ROBERT J. BLAKE
Fledgling
Philomel Books

I am the one
who must go first.

I am afraid.

I set my feet.

I shake my wings.

I jump off into the air.

I only made it
to a ledge.
But I almost
flew.

I set my feet
again.
I shake my wings.
I push off
into the air.

I can do it.

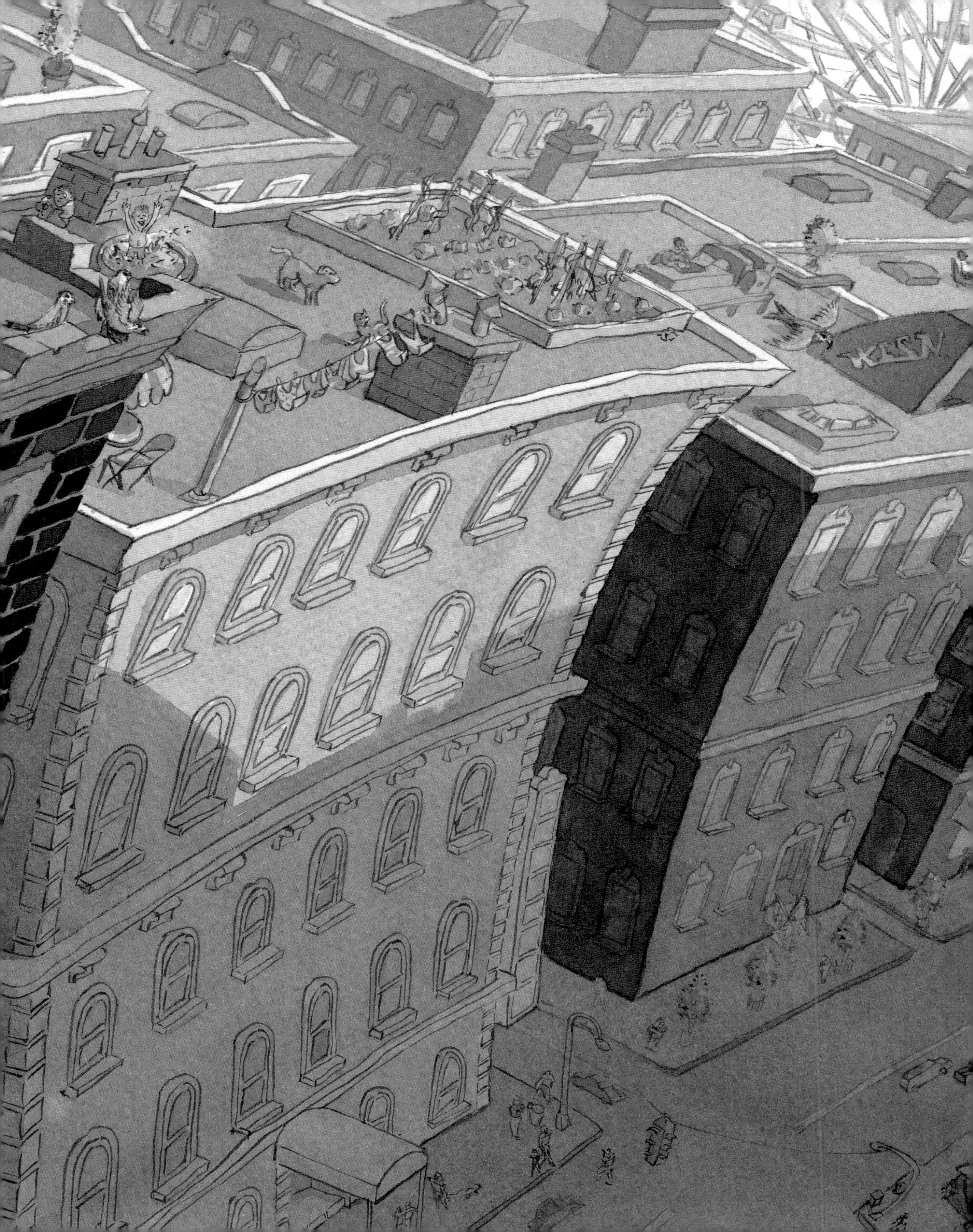

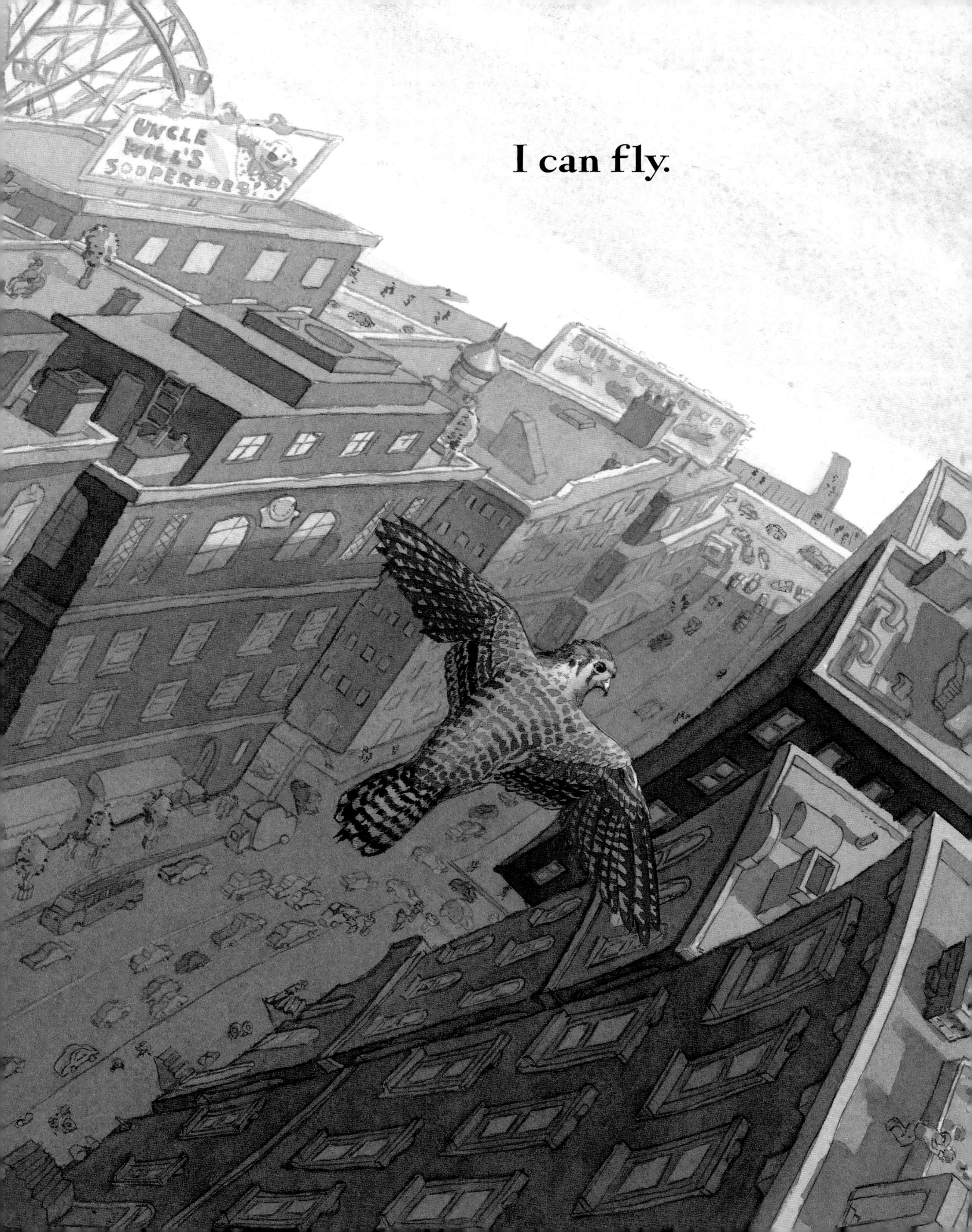

I can fly.

Suddenly,
there is something
behind me.

PIZ

It is a hawk

and it is after me.

I must find somewhere
that it will not go.

Down here?

WILLIE B'S

UPTOWN
D

In here?

THE ★ CITY NEWS
THE ONLY SOURCE YOU NEED
#2
DEREK!

Not here!

BUG
1 A 1
UPTOWN

Out of here.

But now I am lost.
Where is home?

I hear my family call, *Kiy-kiy.*
I answer, *Kiy-kiy.*

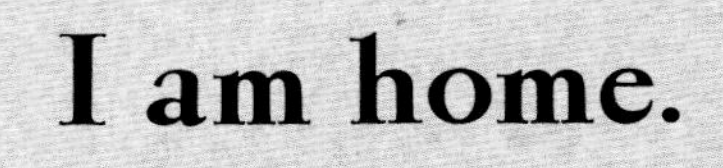

I am home.

To Gary Santolo,

may we never
let our dreams pass us by.

ARTIST'S NOTE

One day I went for a walk with my family and my longtime friend Gary. I'd become a writer and artist, and he'd pursued the study of birds. Suddenly he pointed up and said, "Look, there's a falcon. It's a kestrel." What a coincidence! I'd been fascinated by falcons as a child. I asked him about the beautiful bird. "The American kestrel *(Falco sparverius)* is the smallest falcon found in North America. They eat large insects, small birds, mice. They nest in holes in trees, cliffs, and on buildings."

"Even in the city?" I asked. That intrigued me.

"Yes," he said.

Right then and there I decided to create a book about a falcon's first flight. In a city!

To create *Fledgling*, I corresponded with Gary and visited the Raptor Trust in New Jersey's Great Swamp, where wounded or maimed birds are housed and nursed back to health. Many times I visited. Then, for two months I made pen and ink drawings in my sketchbook of falcons in every conceivable position: walking, eating, cleaning their feathers, flying, landing. I got to know the falcon as I never had. I also walked and sketched the streets of Brooklyn, including the amusement park called Coney Island.

Ideas began to weave into a story. Finally, I made a practice book, called a dummy, telling the story in both words and sketches. When it was time to begin the finished art, I turned to ink and watercolors. I was ready for my story of the falcon to come alive.

—Robert J. Blake

PATRICIA LEE GAUCH, EDITOR.

Published simultaneously in Canada. Printed in Hong Kong by South China Printing Co. (1988) Ltd.
Book design by Semadar Megged. The text is set in 26-point Narcissus Solid.
Library of Congress Cataloging-in-Publication Data
Blake, Robert J. Fledgling / Robert J. Blake. p. cm.
Summary: When a young kestrel makes its first flight among the buildings of a city, it is pursued by a hawk.
1. Kestrels—Juvenile fiction. [1. Kestrels—Fiction. 2. City and town life—Fiction.]
I. Title. PZ10.3.B5815 Fl 2000 [E]—dc21 99-054838
ISBN 0-399-23321-0
1 3 5 7 9 10 8 6 4 2
First Impression

Sing to the Stars

by
Mary Brigid Barrett

Illustrated by
Sandra Speidel

Little, Brown and Company
Boston New York Toronto London

Ephram walks sprightly down the street. Head high, he swings his black case back and forth, to and fro.

Girls jump rope as Ephram strides by. They hop, they skip, jump, jumping. Beaded and bowed, their braids fly high. Up and down, up and down. The rope slaps the sidewalk, *plat, plat, plat*.

FSQ

It's late afternoon. Mr. Washington steps out of his Laundromat, his dog's harness in one hand, his toolbox in the other. He eases himself into a folding chair. Bending forward, he touches his dog, nose to wet nose. Shiloh licks his chin and cheeks. Chuckling, Mr. Washington wipes his face with a big plaid handkerchief. His hand pat, pat, pats his dog and his foot tap, tap, taps the cracked cement.

"How are you today, Ephram?"

Ephram stops. “Evening to you, Mr. Washington,” he says, thumping his case against his leg. “Hello there, Shiloh.” He pauses. “Mr. Washington, sir, how do you always know it’s me walking by?”

“Well, son, every walk’s got a rhythm. My ears tell me light step, brush, light step, brush, must be Ephram walking home from his violin lesson, stepping glad and swinging his violin case.”

"You can tell I'm happy by the sound of my walk?" asks Ephram.

"Boy, I can tell when your violin teacher has been razzing you and you're full up pitiful with yourself!"

"Really?"

"Oh yes, your shoes clap the cement slow and dull. Your case thuds low against your leg. But that's rare, Ephram. Most times you walk with the song of life in your step. You must make sweet music on that violin. Your grandma says you've got a gift."

"Don't know about that, Mr. Washington," says Ephram. "But I do like to play this violin. It speaks when I haven't got any words. I like to practice after supper, up on the roof."

Mr. Washington smiles broadly. He reaches for Ephram's hand. "Here I thought it was old Mr. Bach, sliding down his 'Jesu, Joy of Man's Desiring' from his heavenly station. And all the time it was you, Ephram, up on that roof."

Ephram pulls his hand away from Mr. Washington. "You heard me on the roof? I thought nobody could hear me out there."

"I keep my apartment windows open in this heat," says Mr. Washington, pointing up toward the windows above the Laundromat. "I heard you playing last night. A breeze swept your music down from the roof, and boy, you play to take my breath away.

"There's a neighborhood concert in the park tomorrow night, a fundraiser for a new playground. It's an open mike. Anyone can play. How 'bout it, Ephram?"

UNDRY

Ephram steps back from Mr. Washington. "A stage and all those people, I — I just don't know," he stammers, clutching his violin case tight against his chest. "I've got to go now, Mr. Washington. Grandma will be keeping supper."

"Good-bye, Ephram." Grabbing Shiloh's harness, Mr. Washington stands. "Remember, Ephram," he calls, "music speaks best when someone listens."

Ephram walks on. Past the rap group on the corner. Past the boom box blaring. Past the glaring neon signs flashing on-off, on-off.

"Hey, man, get yourself an electric guitar!" yells one of the group.

Ephram swings around and fingers his violin case as if he were playing a guitar. Then he slaps the case, spins it, and raises it up onto his shoulder, playing it with an imaginary bow. The rapper flashes him a thumbs-up signal. Smiling, Ephram nods back.

Ephram ducks into his building. Pots and pans clank and clatter through thin walls. Televisions blare. A baby squalls. The air is hot and still in the hallways.

"Grandma, I'm home," says Ephram.

"Hello, Sugar," she says. She wipes the sweat from Ephram's brow and kisses him on top of his head. "Supper's ready. Did you have a fine lesson?"

"Yes. I stopped and talked to Mr. Washington on the way home. I think he knows music, Grandma."

"You bet he knows music, Sugar. Mr. Washington was a professional."

"He was?" says Ephram, sitting down to eat.

"Yes, indeed. Mr. Washington trained as a classical pianist. He was your grandfather's and my neighbor when we were young and living in Harlem. One sweltering summer night we were all invited upstairs to a rent party in our building. Mr. James P. Johnson was there, his hands pounding on the piano keys, one hand playing the rhythms of New Orleans, the other making the keys sing the song of New York. Our music pulsated through the air on that sultry night. From then on Flash Fingers Washington played hot, joyful jazz and cool, soulful blues. You should have heard him play, Ephram," says Grandma. "His fingers flew across the keys. Any piece of music, classical, jazz, old spirituals, he gave it style."

"Grandma, he never told me he could play an instrument. Does he play anymore?"

"Not since he and his little girl were in a car accident. That's when Mr. Washington lost his sight."

"His little girl, Grandma, what happened to his little girl?"

Grandma wraps her arms tight around him. "His little girl died in the accident. I suppose he just lost all his joy. He hasn't played since."

Ephram pushes his plate away. His chair scrapes across the floor as he leaves the table.

"Where are you going?" asks Grandma. "You haven't finished your supper."

Ephram picks up his violin. "I need to practice, Grandma."

Up on the roof, the hubbub bustle of cars and people fades to a murmur. In the twilight, Ephram plays his violin, and its sweet song floats out into the wide night.

The next morning Ephram dresses quickly and runs to the park, his feet beating the sidewalk fast time. The stage is set for the concert. Microphones and amplifiers are tested one, two, three, four. On the stage floor, Ephram sees a piano.

He pauses, then walks on, steady, determined, straight to Mr. Washington's Laundromat.

"You're up early this morning, Ephram."

"I don't have my violin case today, Mr. Washington. How d'you —"

"How did I know it was you? Well, son," says Mr. Washington, unlocking the coin box on the dryer. "I told you before, you've got the song of life in your step. This morning it sounds like you're as bold as Mr. Louis Armstrong's horn laying down the 'Tiger Rag.' "

"Mr. Washington," says Ephram, "I've been thinking about playing at the benefit concert tonight. It'd be an honor to play with Flash Fingers Washington."

"Your grandma told you?"

"Yes, sir."

"Ephram, it's been years since I've played." Placing his hands on a laundry table, Mr. Washington spreads his fingers wide, lifting each one individually, clasping and unclasping his hands. "I don't even know if these hands can make a piano sing anymore, Ephram. And I'm not sure I want to find out."

Ephram slips his hands into Mr. Washington's. "Just come, Mr. Washington. The concert begins at eight o'clock."

At the benefit concert, neighbors greet each other. Parents tap their feet and children clap hands to the music. Ephram sits next to his grandmother, his violin case on his lap. "Do you think Mr. Washington will come, Grandma?" asks Ephram.

"Yes . . . yes, I do believe he'll come," says Grandma. "Save this seat for him, here at the end, so Shiloh can sit right by him."

Ephram looks at his watch, trying to read its face in a beam from the streetlight. "It's too late, Grandma. I told him eight o'clock and it's already past eight-thirty! He would have been here by now."

The group from the corner is rapping onstage. Their drums fill the air with a pulsating beat. Suddenly, the lights go out. There's a loud thump and a clang from onstage. "Power outage," someone yells. Metal chairs clink as people rise then sink back into their seats, some chattering, some shouting, all wondering what to do.

"It's this heat," says Grandma. "Too many air conditioners blowing in this town. A brownout, I think they call it."

Ephram takes out his violin. "It's time for me to play now, Grandma."

"Ephram," says Grandma, "how can you play in the dark?"

A wet nose tickles Ephram's elbow, a hand firmly grasps his shoulder. "It's always dark . . . up on the roof, isn't it, Ephram?"

Mr. Washington smiles. "Evening, Rachel," he says. "Shiloh and I couldn't miss your grandson's neighborhood debut. Hope we're not too late."

"It's never too late, Balthazar Washington," says Grandma.

“Mr. Washington, people are beginning to leave. I’m going onstage to play some of the old songs Grandma sings in church. There’s a piano onstage. Will you play with me, sir?”

Mr. Washington tightens his grip on Shiloh’s harness and sits down on the empty chair. He pulls out his handkerchief and wipes the sweat from his face and neck.

“Mr. Washington,” says Ephram, “music speaks best when someone listens.”

Mr. Washington turns toward Ephram’s voice. “Shiloh, you stay here with my friend Rachel. Ephram and ole Flash Fingers Washington, we gonna make some sweet sounds tonight.”

Ephram grins widely. “Do you know ‘Amazing Grace,’ Mr. Washington?”

“Ephram, I was playing ‘Amazing Grace’ when you were a thought in the good Lord’s mind!” Mr. Washington places his hand on Ephram’s forearm. “Ready, son?”

“Be careful getting up on that stage, you two,” cautions Grandma.

“Don’t worry, Grandma,” says Ephram. “Mr. Washington sees in the dark.”

Up on the stage, Ephram seats Mr. Washington at the piano. The crowd buzzes. Ephram shoulders his violin. He raises his bow and begins "Amazing Grace." Mr. Washington joins in. The hum of the crowd fades, and in the darkness the music sings to the stars.

For Dick, with love:
"Where a lone man may be overcome, two together can resist.
A three-ply cord is not easily broken."
Ecclesiastes 4:12
— M.B.B.

To my daughter Zoe, who was born under a lucky star, and to our friend Robert Garth Williams.
— S.S.

First Edition

Library of Congress Cataloging-in-Publication Data

Barrett, Mary Brigid.
Sing to the stars / by Mary Brigid Barrett ; illustrated by Sandra Speidel. — 1st ed.
p. cm.
Summary: When Ephram becomes friends with a blind man in his neighborhood and finds out that Mr. Washington was a famous pianist who hasn't touched a piano for a long time, he resolves to get the man back on stage.
ISBN 0-316-08224-4
[1. Blind — Fiction. 2. Physically handicapped — Fiction. 3. Pianists — Fiction. 4. Friendship — Fiction. 5. Afro-Americans — Fiction.] I. Speidel, Sandra, ill. II. Title.
PZ7.B275343Si 1994
[Fic] — dc20 92-41773

10 9 8 7 6 5 4 3 2 1

NIL

Published simultaneously in Canada
by Little, Brown & Company (Canada) Limited

Printed in Italy